DR. DRABBLE, GENIUS INVENTOR
Dr. Drabble's Incredible Identical Robot Innovation
Dr. Drabble's Phenomenal Antigravity Dust Machine
Dr. Drabble's Remarkable Underwater Breathing Pills
Dr. Drabble's Astounding Musical Mesmerizer
Dr. Drabble's Spectacular Shrinker-Enlarger
Dr. Drabble's Amazing Invisibility Mirror
Dr. Drabble's Wondrous Weather Dispenser
Dr. Drabble's Fantastic Fanfaring Finder

DR. DRABBLE'S
SPECTACULAR SHRINKER-
ENLARGER

Written by
Sigmund Brouwer and Wayne Davidson
Illustrated by
Bill Bell

VICTOR BOOKS®
A DIVISION OF SCRIPTURE PRESS PUBLICATIONS INC.
USA CANADA ENGLAND

To John and Emily

The travels with their missionary parents had led PJ and Chelsea, along with their pet skunk Wesley, to the South American country of Brazil.

One morning, they ventured to the marketplace with Dr. Drabble, the genius inventor who took all of them around the world on his Brilliant All-in-One Traveling Apparatus.

"Aren't these people strange?" Chelsea said as they walked.

"Yes," PJ replied. "They dress and talk funny and have different skin."

Dr. Drabble heard every word they said, but decided to remain quiet. He led them farther into the marketplace and they saw many more strange things.

ISBN: 0-89693-969-3

© 1992 SP Publications, Inc. All rights reserved.

VICTOR BOOKS
A division of SP Publications, Inc.
Wheaton, Illinois 60187

The strangest thing they saw were the twin brothers behind a coffee-bean stand.

"We sell the rare cocoa-coffee beans," they called. "They're the best. Buy from us."

They were so strange that Chelsea began to giggle loudly.

"PJ, look at those two men!"

Dr. Drabble still said nothing.

PJ giggled as well. "It looks like they have bananas for noses."

Chelsea thought that was so funny, she fell to the ground laughing.

One of the twin brothers helped her stand again. "Are you all right?" he asked.

Chelsea stared right at his nose again. She and PJ laughed harder.

"It's just that you look so funny," she said. "We can't help ourselves."

Dr. Drabble shook his head sadly, then led the children away.

"Where are you taking us?" PJ asked. "It's so fun to see all these strange people."

"Back to the laboratory on the Brilliant All-in-One Traveling Apparatus," Dr. Drabble said firmly. "It's a good time to show you my new invention."

When they returned, Dr. Drabble announced it proudly.

"Tah-dah! My Spectacular Shrinker-Enlarger."

PJ and Chelsea did not have to ask what it did. They could see the results in front of them.

"Where's Arnie Clodbuckle?" Chelsea asked. "Since he's your assistant, he should be right here."

"He went looking for a watermelon," Dr. Drabble explained. "I want to do some more experiments."

Sure enough, Arnie arrived a short time later.

"Hold still," Dr. Drabble said. "Let me aim the Spectacular Shrinker-Enlarger at the watermelon."

Arnie stood in the middle of the room and closed his eyes.

Dr. Drabble fiddled with some switches on the Spectacular Shrinker-Enlarger.

ZAAAAAP! He shot a ray toward Arnie.

When Arnie opened his eyes again, the watermelon was very tiny in his hands.

"The watermelon shrank!" he shouted with glee.

"Oh dear," Dr. Drabble clucked. "Not only did I hit the wrong button, but my aim was wrong."

Then Arnie realized that Dr. Drabble had enlarged him instead of shrinking the watermelon.

"EEEEP!" Arnie cried in a deep voice.

"Don't worry," Dr. Drabble said. "I can easily shrink you."

ZAAAAP! Another ray hit Arnie.

Before Chelsea and PJ could blink, Arnie shrank so small that the watermelon nearly landed on top of his head.

"Ooooh noooooo!" Arnie's little voice reached them. "You enlarged the whole room."

Dr. Drabble sighed. Arnie never was good at thinking.

"No, Arnie," he said. "I just shrank you too much. Hold still and let me try again."

"Hurry! Please hurry!" Arnie cried. "I don't know if Wesley wants me to be his friend or his lunch!"

Arnie scrambled up Dr. Drabble's leg to reach the tabletop.

"We can dress you up in doll clothes," Chelsea suggested.

"Oh, please hurry," Arnie asked. "That's worse than Wesley."

On the next try, Dr. Drabble hit the right switch on the Spectacular Shrinker-Enlarger. ZAAAAP!

Arnie zoomed up to his normal size. "Thank you," he said. "For a while, I was worried I would need a ladder to get into bed tonight."

PJ and Chelsea thought it was all great fun. "Enlarge us!"

Dr. Drabble remembered how they had laughed at the twin brothers with the big noses.

"Sure," he said with a sly grin. "Close your eyes."

ZAAAP! ZAAAP!

Two more rays shot out from the Spectacular Shrinker-Enlarger.

PJ opened his eyes and saw that Chelsea had ears like an elephant.

Chelsea opened her eyes and saw that PJ's feet and hands were as big as frying pans.

They began to laugh at each other.

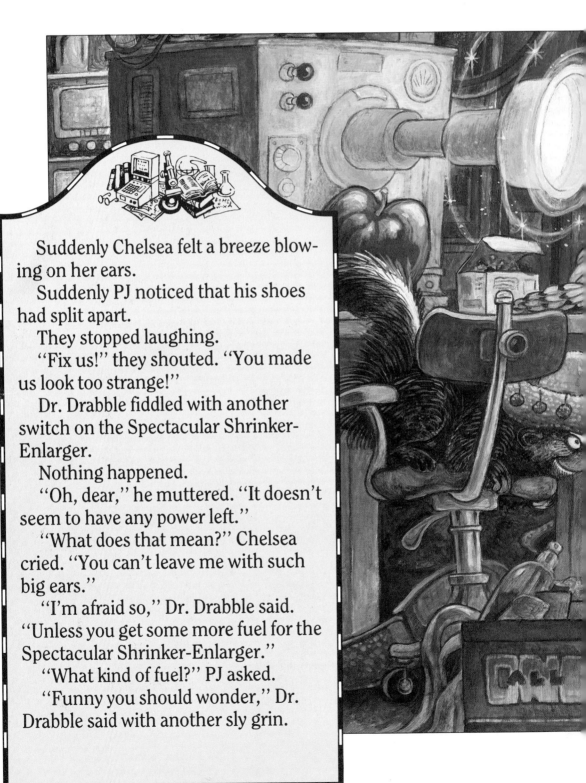

Suddenly Chelsea felt a breeze blowing on her ears.

Suddenly PJ noticed that his shoes had split apart.

They stopped laughing.

"Fix us!" they shouted. "You made us look too strange!"

Dr. Drabble fiddled with another switch on the Spectacular Shrinker-Enlarger.

Nothing happened.

"Oh, dear," he muttered. "It doesn't seem to have any power left."

"What does that mean?" Chelsea cried. "You can't leave me with such big ears."

"I'm afraid so," Dr. Drabble said. "Unless you get some more fuel for the Spectacular Shrinker-Enlarger."

"What kind of fuel?" PJ asked.

"Funny you should wonder," Dr. Drabble said with another sly grin.

Dr. Drabble reminded them of the twin brothers with the big noses. "The Spectacular Shrinker-Enlarger needs more of their rare cocoa-coffee beans."

"Will you quickly send Arnie?" Chelsea asked.

"I can't," Dr. Drabble said. "I think you need to learn a lesson about making fun of people."

"You mean you want *us* to go?" PJ's voice quivered. "Everyone will laugh at us."

Dr. Drabble nodded.

"We'd rather stay in our room," Chelsea said. And they did.

They soon discovered that big ears and big hands and big feet made life difficult.

Sounds were too loud to Chelsea and her ears always got in her way.

PJ tripped every time he walked, and his socks didn't fit.

"I'm afraid we'll have to go outside," PJ finally said. "I don't want enlarged hands and feet for the rest of my life."

Chelsea pulled her ear free from the closet door. "Let's go quickly then."

It was hard for them to run, however. PJ's feet were clumsy, and Chelsea had to be careful that her ears did not get caught on anything.

Worse, every person who saw them laughed out loud.

PJ and Chelsea finally reached the rare cocoa-coffee-bean stand.

"We need help," Chelsea sobbed. "May we have some beans?"

"Yes," PJ added, "and we will understand if you now make fun of us for looking so strange."

The twin brothers looked at each other so quickly that they nearly banged noses.

"Oh, no," the first one said. "How could we make fun of you?"

"What do you mean?" Chelsea asked.

"Well," the second one said, "we know what it feels like to have people laughing at us. Even if we look different, we don't *feel* different from anyone else."

"You may have as many beans as you need," the first twin said kindly. "In fact, we'll even design burlap sacks for you so that people won't laugh anymore."

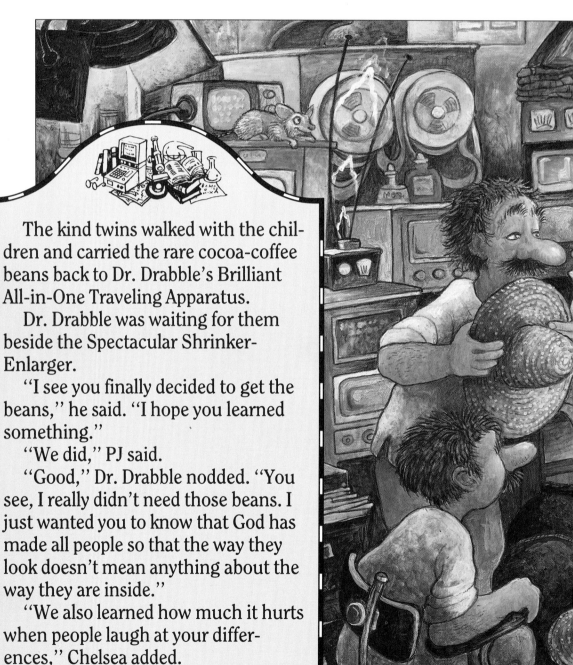

The kind twins walked with the children and carried the rare cocoa-coffee beans back to Dr. Drabble's Brilliant All-in-One Traveling Apparatus.

Dr. Drabble was waiting for them beside the Spectacular Shrinker-Enlarger.

"I see you finally decided to get the beans," he said. "I hope you learned something."

"We did," PJ said.

"Good," Dr. Drabble nodded. "You see, I really didn't need those beans. I just wanted you to know that God has made all people so that the way they look doesn't mean anything about the way they are inside."

"We also learned how much it hurts when people laugh at your differences," Chelsea added.

Dr. Drabble smiled.

ZAAP! ZAAP! ZAAP! ZAAP!

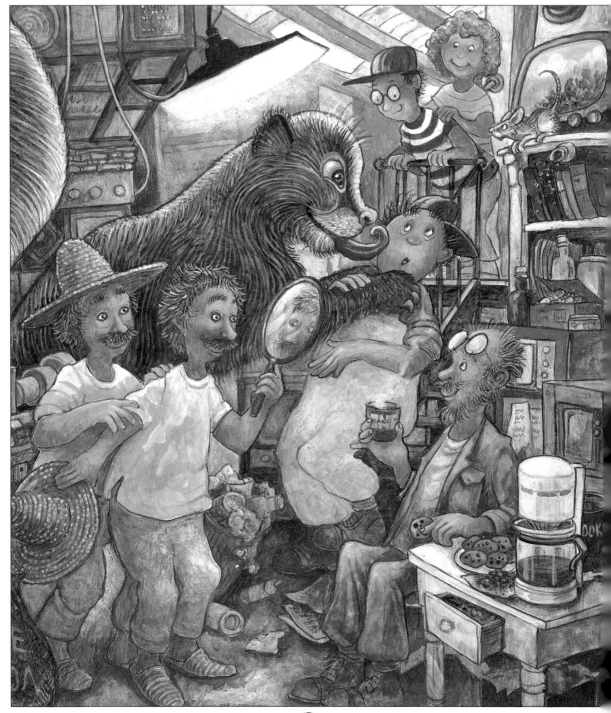